Black Pearl Ponies

The BLACK PEARL PONIES series:

SNICKERS

JENNY OLDFIELD

Illustrated by
JOHN GREEN

Hodder
Children's
Books

A division of Hachette Children's Books

Hodder Children's Books
A division of Hachette Children's Books
338 Euston Road, London NW1 3BH
An Hachette UK company
www.hachette.co.uk

Once more with thanks to the Foster family and all my friends at Lost Valley Ranch, and this time with special thanks to Katie Foster, horse trainer and all-round equine expert.

CHAPTER ONE

Silence! Nothing stirred. Keira sat in the saddle and looked down on the Black Pearl ponies standing like statues in the dewy meadow.

The sun rose and cast its golden light on the ridge above Dolphin Rock, and as the sky turned blue she saw the last pale slice of moon sink behind the mountains.

'OK, elk – where are you?' she murmured.

Red Star shifted gently then took a few steps

towards a stand of aspens higher up the hill. He tossed his head and snorted; *look – over there!*

Sure enough, a bull elk came out from under the trees then stood gazing calmly at Keira and Red Star.

'Wow!' breathed Keira. His antlers were massive. He turned his beautiful head and waited. Soon two females followed him out into the open.

Bang! Down in the valley, a barn door swung

2

shut. A truck engine roared.

The bull elk stiffened. He raised his head and listened.

Bang! This time it was a gate, followed by the chug of the engine across the meadow and then the clatter of hay bales being tipped into metal feeders.

The timid elk had heard enough. They turned and trotted away, back into the aspens, where they quickly disappeared from view.

'At least we saw them!' Keira sighed. She'd got up before dawn especially to catch a glimpse of the rare, shy creatures. 'Good job, Red Star – you were the one who spotted them.'

Red Star tossed his white mane and pranced on the spot. He loved compliments.

'OK, now breakfast!' she grinned, squeezing his

sides and setting him off at a lope along the Jeep road.

'One bull elk and two females!' Keira reported to her mom, dad and older sister, Brooke, as she tucked into her bacon sandwich. 'The sound of the feed truck scared them off, but I saw them clear as day.'

'There's good grazing land in the clearing by Dolphin Rock,' her dad, Jacob, pointed out. He'd already been hard at work feeding the horses and he had a busy Saturday ahead of him so he made himself a second sandwich.

'His antlers were massive! I mean – huge!'

'Keira, did you give Red Star his morning feed?' Allyson, her mom, asked.

'I sure did. I took him into the stalls and gave him

a manger full of yummy alfalfa. You should've come with us this morning, Brooke. You wouldn't believe how beautiful the elk were.'

'And miss my beauty sleep?' Brooke joked. 'Anyway, it's April. The temperature is still below zero at that time in the morning – too cold for me.' She pointed through the window at frost in the meadow and on the red barn roof, and at the snow on the distant peaks.

'OK, is everyone done with breakfast?' Allyson Lucas got them organised as usual. She stacked cutlery and plates in the dishwasher and shooed the others on to the porch. 'Brooke, check on the grain situation so we can put in an order for next Friday. Keira, it's your turn to sweep out the tack room . . .'

'. . . And I'm fixing fences out by the creek.' Jacob jumped up and grabbed his Stetson from its hook.

'Nope – you're first in line to greet Mike and Rex Martin, so you need to clean up,' Allyson reminded him. 'We're taking Rex in as a guest while his dad flies to Europe on business. They're due here in ten minutes, in case you'd forgotten.'

Mike Martin was a wealthy new client from Blowing Rock in Sharman County. He was bringing in two ponies for Jacob to work with and it was important to make a good impression. So while her dad grumbled about having to 'clean up', Keira ran across the yard and got busy in the tack room, growing excited as she thought about the two new arrivals.

This was one of the magical bits about the horse

training operation here at Black Pearl Ranch – that moment when new ponies stepped out of their trailers and took a first, wary look around the corral at the round pen and barn, with the meadow and the creek beyond. Keira loved to see them prick up their ears and take in the beautiful surroundings. Then she would help her dad lead them into the stalls and give them grain. Soon after would come the *munch-munch* sound of happy horses!

'So where are they?' Brooke appeared on the tack room porch, tapping her watch.

Still in a world of her own, Keira laid down her broom. 'Who?'

'The Martins. They're late.'

Just then the girls heard a vehicle cross the cattle guard at the top of the hill. They looked up eagerly at a white truck pulling a shiny silver trailer. It kicked up dirt and raised clouds of dust as it approached.

'Dad!' Keira ran across the yard. 'They're here!'

Just in time to greet the newcomers, Jacob stepped out of the house in his best black hat, a pressed red shirt, clean jeans and his newest boots.

'Wow, you even shaved!' she gasped then dodged as he lunged at her with a fake karate chop – hah-so!

Soon Mike Martin pulled up by the corral and jumped out of the truck. He was tall and serious-looking and was followed out of the cab by a skinny kid with jet black hair. He was Keira's age, dressed in dark blue T-shirt and jeans.

'You must be Jacob,' Martin said, holding out a

broad hand and giving a firm handshake. 'I'm Mike and this is my boy, Rex, who'll be bunking down with you for a couple of weeks.'

Keira's dad smiled at Rex, who blushed then smiled back. 'Good to meet you, sir,' he told Jacob, copying his dad's handshake.

So come on, let's cut the chat and open the trailer! Keira hovered impatiently by the back door.

'These two are the real deal,' Mike was telling Jacob. 'I co-own them with Jeff Baker, who ran for state governor a while back. They're both siblings of the national barrel-racing champion. We paid over two hundred thousand dollars per horse.'

Jacob whistled through his teeth then nodded. 'We'll take real good care of them,' he promised the proud owner.

Come on! Keira thought again. She didn't care what the ponies were worth – all she wanted was to let them out of the trailer. *Open up, please!*

'Vegas is the dark bay colt – real pretty,' Mike explained as he unbolted the door. 'And Snickers is the brown and white paint filly. I warn you – she bites and kicks. I need you to cure her of those bad habits, Jacob.'

Nodding again, Keira's dad stepped into the trailer and led out a colt that was so dark brown he was almost black, except for a white star on his forehead. His coat shone and his mane and tail glistened, and he high-stepped out of the trailer with his neck arched and his head held high, as if he knew that he was worth almost a quarter of a million dollars.

'Wow!' First the elk, now this spectacular colt – it was Keira's day to be wowed off her feet. Eagerly she took Vegas' lead rope from her dad and tethered him to the nearest rail.

'Stand back,' Rex warned when she returned to the trailer. He put out his arm to stop her from getting too close. 'Snickers needs plenty of room.'

So Keira's first view of Snickers was from a

distance. The paint pony was delicately built and beautifully marked with a chestnut brown head and patches of brown across her back and under her belly. The rest was snowy white, along with her mane and tail.

'So pretty!' Brooke sighed, standing beside Keira.

'And she knows it,' Rex told them abruptly. 'Dad and his business partner bought her for me to ride. We aim to get to national level with her.'

'Barrel racing?' Brooke asked. She and Keira entered fun local competitions where each rider wove in and out of a line of painted oil barrels in the fastest possible time. Red Star and Keira often came away with first prize.

Rex nodded. Like his dad, he was unsmiling and a bit intense. 'Snickers is the real reason we're here.'

Keira let Brooke carry on with the conversation while she took in every beautiful detail of the paint pony's appearance. 'How come?' Brooke asked.

'Like Dad said, she has a mean streak – you shouldn't go too near her.'

No way – I don't believe it! Keira thought. Her dad was tethering Snickers to the rail alongside Vegas

14

and she wasn't acting up the least little bit.

'Your dad is the fourth trainer we've used,' Rex told them with a frown. 'The others tried everything they knew to cure her, but nothing worked.'

'Did the vet check out her mouth?' Brooke wanted to know. 'If she bites, maybe there's a problem with her teeth.'

'Or her feet if she kicks,' Keira added. Any good farrier would take a look and know what to do.

Rex sighed. 'Yeah, course, we did all that.'

'Well, if anyone can stop her biting and kicking, it's Dad!' Brooke said breezily as Keira tuned in to the conversation between Jacob and Mike Martin.

'We'll pay you for a two-week intensive training programme,' Mike was saying. 'Vegas will be no problem – you just need to put some miles on him out on the trails and build up the basic aids. And Rex will be here to ride Snickers, so any techniques you can put his way will be welcome.'

'Sure,' Jacob replied. 'These are two fine ponies – it'll be fun working with them.'

The men shook hands and Allyson came out of the house, ready to show Rex to his room. Brooke had gone off into the tack room but Keira was still drooling over Vegas and Snickers.

'I can't decide who I like best – you're both pretty cool,' she murmured, stroking each in turn.

Vegas arched his neck. Snickers whinnied softly. *We're more than cool*, they seemed to say.

'OK then – you're totally gorgeous!' Keira said with a laugh as she led them into the barn. 'Dad's right – working with you two is going to be fun!'

CHAPTER TWO

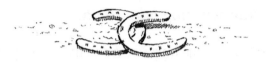

'Did you see what Rex did?' Brooke whispered late that night. She and Keira were in her bedroom overlooking the moonlit yard. They kept their voices low.

'When Dad asked him to hose down the saddle blankets, he snuck off into the barn to use his laptop!'

Keira nodded. 'And when Mom asked him to help with the dishes after supper, he disappeared again!'

'Plus, he refused to scoop poop in the corral!'

'And where was he when we had to lay straw in Snickers' stall?'

The two sisters had a lot to get off their chests. All day they'd run around picking up the chores that Rex had been supposed to do.

'OK, son, I have a plane to catch,' Mike Martin had said once Snickers and Vegas were safely installed. 'Time to say goodbye.'

There'd been no hugs, nothing. Rex had just grabbed his bag from the trailer, slung it over his shoulder and walked away.

'See you in two weeks,' his dad had called after him.

It was Allyson who'd fussed over Rex and made sure he had everything he needed, Allyson who'd said they were happy to have him as part of the team at Black Pearl. 'Though I have to warn you that we all work hard around here,' she'd warned. 'And we'll be expecting you to do your fair share.'

'Sure thing, ma'am,' Rex had replied respectfully.

But as soon as Allyson's back had been turned, Rex had used every trick in the book to wriggle out of work. 'I don't scoop poop and I don't clean tack!' he'd declared to Keira and Brooke. 'Back home at Blowing Rock we employ a guy full time to do that stuff.'

'But the kid eats and eats!' Brooke reminded Keira, holed up in her room. 'At supper he asked for second helpings before I even got started.'

'And he hogged the TV and chose the

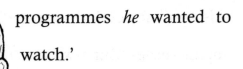

programmes *he* wanted to watch.'

'And he pigged out on all the cookies we baked yesterday.'

'Yeah,' Keira sighed. She gazed out of the window at the starlit sky and the moon shining over the mountains. At the end of day one, it hadn't been the expensive horses who were the problem, but Rex. She yawned then stood up, ready to tiptoe off to her own room. 'And he's sneaky with it.'

'Real polite to Mom and Dad,' Brooke agreed. 'But as soon as they turn their backs he turns into this spoiled-rich-kid monster.' She gave Keira a rueful smile. 'But tomorrow's a new day, right? Maybe Rex will cowboy up.'

Keira shook her head. 'Or maybe he'll wimp out for two whole weeks,' she muttered as she went off to bed.

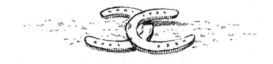

'Where's Rex?' Jacob asked at eight-thirty the next morning.

'Still in bed,' Keira told him.

'I thought he wanted to work with his filly.' Her dad had already saddled Snickers and led her into the round pen where Keira and Vegas had joined him. This was their first chance to put the ponies through their paces and Jacob was keen to pick up

21

any possible problem. 'Honey, why don't you hop up on Vegas and let me take a look.'

Carefully Keira eased her foot into Vegas' left stirrup and slid her right leg over the saddle. The dark bay colt snorted but soon settled under her weight.

'How does he feel?' Jacob asked, holding Snickers on a short rope.

'Good.' Keira wanted to ask Vegas to back up so she tightened her reins and leaned forward to ease her weight out of the saddle. The colt took three steps back before she relaxed the reins again. 'Yeah, good!' she decided, working with him for a few more minutes before her dad asked her to switch ponies.

'Whatever Mike said, there doesn't seem to be a big problem with this little lady,' Jacob told her, holding Snickers steady as Keira eased into his saddle. She sat quietly and took up the reins.

The delicate paint pony flicked her ears and waited patiently for Keira to tell her what to do.

'Let's see if you're right,' she said to her dad. 'Same thing to start – let's back up a little,' she told Snickers, leaning forward and tightening the reins. She felt the pony's body quiver and instead of backing up she tried to twist her head towards Keira's left leg. 'No biting!' Keira warned her, holding steady and making her carry out the instruction. 'Nice and easy – one step, two, three – good girl!'

'Good job,' Jacob told her. 'Now walk her forward around the arena.'

Shifting her balance and using pressure from her legs, Keira eased Snickers into a walk. When they were halfway round the circuit, she saw a tousle-headed Rex emerge from the house carrying his laptop. 'Hey!' she called. 'Come and see – your filly's doing good!'

Rex yawned and stretched. Slowly he made his way to the fence. 'Yeah, wait till we try riding her out on the trails,' he warned. 'Snickers is lazy – she hates to work.'

First she bites and kicks, now she's lazy! Keira thought. *How come Rex doesn't have one nice thing to say about his high-value pony?* She was glad when her dad called for her to put Snickers into a trot and then a lope so she could show Rex how well she was doing.

And wow, was she smooth! Her trot was amazing, her lope excellent. And the little paint seemed eager to please. She listened to everything Keira asked her to do and didn't act up once, speeding round and round the arena like a perfect show pony.

'You want to try her around some barrels?' Jacob called to Rex after Keira and Snickers had worked for fifteen minutes.

'No thank you, sir. Maybe tomorrow,' Rex replied, wandering away with his computer.

Keira's dad shrugged. 'I guess he's homesick,' he suggested.

Or maybe he's the lazy one, not Snickers, Keira thought as she dismounted. She led her out of the arena, took off her saddle and bridle, brushed her down then gave her water. 'I still say you're a great pony,' she told her.

Snickers turned her head to look at Keira. *Tell me more!*

'I said you're a terrific girl and you're beautiful!' Keira laughed. 'You and me, we're getting along just fine!'

CHAPTER THREE

'Sunday afternoons we get to relax a little,' Allyson explained to Rex over lunch. 'The girls plan on riding out along the Jeep road towards Three Horseshoes Ranch. Why don't you and Snickers join them?'

'Yeah, cool,' Rex said in a flat voice. 'Snickers is sure to act up out on the trail, but I can handle it.'

'We usually meet up with Reed Walters and ride by the creek,' Brooke explained. 'Reed rides an

Appaloosa named Wildflower. You'll really like her.'

But after lunch, when Snickers, Red Star and Brooke's pony, Annie, were tacked up and ready to go, Rex was nowhere to be found.

'Go look in the barn,' Brooke suggested with a sigh.

So Keira ran across the corral and into the barn, peering in at Vegas to check he was happy in his stall and finally finding Rex holed up with his computer in Snickers' empty stall next door. He was Skyping his parents and was deep in conversation.

'Mom, it's not fair,' he complained. 'You're paying for me to be here and all they do is make me work.'

Keira gasped. She stayed hidden behind the stall door.

'I'm up at dawn scooping poop and polishing tack. And the food here is terrible. They're trying to starve me.'

'Oh, honey – I'm so sorry,' the woman on the screen replied. She was sitting in a hotel room, using hair-straighteners on her glossy dark hair as she talked. 'But hey, it's only for a couple of weeks while your dad and I are in London.'

'The Lucases are way too strict,' Rex moaned. 'And the kids here – Brooke and Keira – they think they're hot-shot riders and all they do is go nose to tail on their dumb trail ponies. It's boring!'

'Only two weeks,' Mrs Martin reminded him.

Another figure appeared on screen behind her. Mike Martin stooped to come into view. 'How's Jacob doing with the ponies?' he asked.

Huddled over his laptop, Rex scowled. 'He hasn't even started working with them,' he lied to his dad. 'It's me – I'm having to do all the work. He's forcing me to ride Snickers out on the trail this afternoon, even though you told him how mean she is.'

Now Keira gritted her teeth. It was all she could do to stop herself bursting into the stall and telling the Martins the truth.

On screen Mike looked concerned. 'You call us back later,' he ordered his son as he knotted his tie. 'Let me know how it goes.'

'But be nice, Rex,' Mrs Martin insisted. 'We brought you up to remember your manners at all times, even if you're mad at someone.'

'OK,' Rex grunted. 'But I'm telling you – this isn't a good place. Whatever you heard about Jacob Lucas running the best training facility in the county – it's not true.'

That was it – Keira had heard enough. She flung open the stall door and said in a loud voice, 'Hey, Rex – Dad saddled your filly. We're ready to go.'

'I'm on my way,' Rex muttered, blushing as he logged off and refusing to look Keira in the eye.

He knows I heard! Keira told herself. She strode out of the barn without looking round, her stomach churning and her face flushed with anger. *How can he do that – tell his parents downright lies and be all nicey-nicey to Mom and Dad's faces? I mean, how much worse can this get?*

Much worse, as it turned out.

'So how come Snickers went through three other trainers?' Reed Walters wanted to know. Brooke had filled him in on the filly's background as they rode by the creek. Rex and Snickers lagged behind so Reed had reined Wildflower back to wait for them.

'Some horses are born mean and she happens to be one of them,' Rex replied. 'But she cost my dad and his partner a heap of money. They need someone to train the meanness out of her before they can sell her on.'

'I thought your dad bought her for you to barrel race in the national championships.' Keira had overheard and held Red Star back. Yet again he was blaming poor Snickers, who at this moment was trying to deal with being out on the trail for the first time. Keira picked up that she was nervous, constantly looking to Wildflower, Red Star and Annie for support.

'That was the idea,' Rex grunted. He jerked sharply at Snickers' reins to stop her from tossing her head. 'But now we know she won't ever make it at that level.'

'Really?' After what Keira had overheard in the barn, she was in the mood to argue. For a start, she refused to believe that any horse was *born* mean. It all depended on how you treated them. 'You saw how Dad and I worked with her in the round pen – she did real well.'

'Yeah, you just wait,' Rex insisted. 'Dad's not ready to admit how bad she is either – he's set on giving it one last shot.'

'That's why you're here?' Reed asked. 'Your dad made a good choice – Jacob Lucas is the best trainer around. He'll soon iron out any kinks.' With a friendly smile and a nod he rode on again to catch up with Brooke and Annie.

For a while Keira rode Red Star in silence. She

let him wander off the trail into the creek, where his hooves splashed through the clear, cold water and clattered against the smooth rocks underfoot.

'Bring Snickers in here,' she suggested at last. 'It's fun.'

'No way – she'll spook big time,' Rex told her, still tugging at the reins and kicking with his spurs to get her to go.

Snickers pulled against the bit and at the same time struggled to pick up pace.

So do you want her to stop or go forwards? Keira wondered. *If you pull at her mouth she thinks you want to slow down. If you kick her she thinks you want to trot. Poor Snickers doesn't know what to do.*

She frowned as she rode until at last she realised something important and she leaned forward to whisper in Red Star's ear. 'You know what, I reckon it's Rex who's spooking big time, not his horse!'

By now, Reed and Brooke were a hundred metres ahead and reaching a bend in the trail. Brooke turned in the saddle. 'How about a game of trot tag?' she called.

'No thanks, but you two go ahead,' Keira yelled back.

'You go join them,' Rex insisted, confusing his pony so badly that she crow hopped on the spot – up-down, up-down, arching her back.

'No, really . . .' Keira hesitated. Part of her wanted to join in the fun, but she knew she should stay behind to keep an eye on Snickers and Rex.

'Go!' Rex repeated with an angry glare. 'I can handle this!'

Keira gritted her teeth. *OK – good!* she thought. *If that's the way you want it.* With that, she set Red Star into a trot to catch up with Brooke and Reed.

But after she trotted round the bend in the trail she had second thoughts. 'So I really couldn't care less what happens to Rex,' she told Red Star, 'but Snickers will be scared stiff if we leave her all alone.'

Red Star agreed. He slowed to a walk and glanced back at Keira as if saying, maybe we ought to go back and check it out?

So Keira neck reined her savvy pony to return the way they'd come. 'Where did they go?' she said as they took the bend at a trot. To her surprise, the trail was empty.

Red Star slowed from trot to walk. He scanned the slope up towards Dolphin Rock then looked down towards the creek. Then he snorted and headed straight for a thicket of willows growing at the water's edge.

Soon Keira saw why. Or rather, she heard the reason Red Star had decided to head this way.

'Quit that!' Rex's voice rose above the sound of water running over rocks. It was followed by a shrill neigh and the splashing of hooves. 'Get out of the creek, you dumb animal!'

Keira swallowed hard. She rode on. Through the silvery green willow leaves she picked out glimpses of Snickers' brown and white coat and the darker shape of her young rider yanking at the reins and kicking hard. 'Go, Red Star!' she urged, aiming to stop Rex from digging those sharp spurs into Snickers' sides.

But things got quickly out of hand. Rex shouted, panicking his filly and making her plunge up to her withers in the creek water. Then she reared on to her hind legs, lost her footing and threw herself sideways towards the bank. Rex grabbed the saddle horn. He was whipped backwards then flung to the side and this is when Keira learned that he was no rodeo rider. She watched him bounce and slide in the saddle, lose his grip on the horn and fly through the air.

Splash. 'Help!'

Keira and Red Star rode clear of the willows to find Snickers already scrambling up the bank to safety.

'Rex!' she yelled, her stomach twisting into a tight knot. 'Where are you?'

'Over here!' he cried, waving his arms wildly.

The call came from downstream and it was a while before Keira spotted him, up to his waist in ice cold water.

'I can't swim!' he yelled, thrashing about and stumbling in even deeper.

'Hold on, we'll get you out,' Keira promised. With her heart beating hard against her ribcage, she rode Red Star into the creek.

CHAPTER FOUR

R ed Star plunged into the water and waded
strongly towards Rex. As soon as they drew
near, Keira leaned sideways and grabbed his arm.
'Hang on,' she said.

'It's cold!' he gasped, clutching her hand.

'We'll soon get you out,' she promised as she
kept a firm hold. The water had reached her boots
and she knew she was in for a soaking. 'Climb up
behind me and hold tight,' she instructed.

Red Star held steady in the rushing water as Rex slithered on to his back, then he turned and slowly waded out of the creek, only stopping when he and Keira had Rex back on dry land.

'Are you OK?' Keira asked. She slid to the ground in her waterlogged boots then helped Rex to dismount.

'I'm c-c-cold!' he wailed.

'OK, my jacket's dry – you can have it,' she told him, taking it off and wrapping it around his shoulders. He was dripping from head to toe and shivering badly.

'D-don't tell anyone about this, please,' Rex begged, huddling inside Keira's jacket.

He glanced at Snickers who had sidled up beside Red Star and was waiting quietly.

'Hmmm, well how do you suggest we explain the drowned-rat look then?' Keira wanted to know. Now that she realised Rex wasn't going to come to any harm, she felt cross again.

'D-don't tell them,' he pleaded through chattering teeth. 'S-say it was a game of tag that went wrong.'

Keira shook her head then thought hard. 'Why

'should I?' she wanted to know.

'Because,' Rex sighed.

'Because . . . what?' Keira glared at him.

'Because I don't want my dad to find out I couldn't handle Snickers,' Rex said under his breath. 'That's why!'

'Off with those wet clothes,' Allyson told Rex the moment she saw him walking Snickers back into the corral.

Brooke and Reed had done a U-turn on the Jeep road and caught up with Keira and Rex and they'd all come home together, Snickers hanging her head as her drenched rider walked alongside.

'She spooked big time over nothing then bolted

into the creek,' Rex had told Reed with a hollow laugh, looking sideways at Keira, who had frowned. She hadn't actually given Rex any promises, yet somehow, when it came to telling the truth her tongue was tied.

'Yeah, she bites and kicks and now she bolts,' Rex complained. 'Terrific, huh?'

Snickers had dropped her head lower still and trudged unhappily towards the ranch.

'Go take a shower then sit by the warm fire,' Allyson told Rex as she removed Snickers' saddle.

'I'll finish here and lead her into her stall,' Keira offered and immediately started work on brushing Snickers down. 'OK, I know it's not fair,' she murmured as the others went off. 'Rex shouldn't get away with blaming you for this.'

Snickers took a deep breath which came out as a sigh. Her deep brown eyes looked sad.

Standing next to her at the rail, Red Star gave the pretty filly a friendly nuzzle.

'I don't know why I kept quiet before, but for a second back there I actually did feel sorry for Rex,' Keira explained as she brushed Snickers' long white mane. 'Guess what – he's a terrible rider but he doesn't want his dad to know that,' she said, slowly thinking her way through the problem.

Snickers turned her head and curled back her soft upper lip to nuzzle Keira's hand.

'See – if you do that to your owner he probably thinks you want to bite him,' she explained. 'I know different – you're just being friendly. But how do you tell that to someone as pig-headed as Rex?'

'Hey Keira, who are you calling pig-headed?' Reed called from across the corral as he mounted Wildflower and got ready to ride home to Three Horseshoes.

She looked up and blushed. 'No one!' she replied. She watched Reed ride away with a cheerful wave then began again with her brush. 'So Snickers, I know it's hard but I guess we have to give Rex one last chance,' she decided, brushing again until the brown on the filly's coat glistened like a new chestnut and the white was pure as snow.

'We've got a deal – OK?' Keira told Rex next morning. She'd rushed through the science lesson her mom had set for her then hurried out to work with her dad, Rex and Snickers in the round pen. 'The deal is – you work hard with your pony on the methods my dad teaches and I won't tell anyone about yesterday.'

Rex knotted his brows, keeping his distance from Snickers as Keira buckled on her head collar.

'No more pulling on her mouth,' she told him. 'And no more kicking with spurs. Deal?'

'Deal,' he muttered as Jacob came out of the tack room ready to work his horsemanship magic.

And they started back at the beginning by sending Snickers round the arena without a rider, trotting her until her head went down and she grew tired.

'See that? Lowering her head is a signal,' Jacob told Rex, who stood with him in the middle of the round pen. 'She's telling you she wants to stop trotting. She knows you're the boss and she wants to come join you.'

'How do you *know* that?' Rex said with a frown.

Jacob smiled and let Snickers slow to a walk. Then he half turned his back on her. 'We know horses don't have words to communicate but they use body language instead. See how her ears are flicked forward. That means her attention is totally on us. She's waiting to be told what to do. Now look away. Don't give her eye contact. That way, she'll come right up to you and ask you.'

'She will?' Rex still wasn't sure, but he turned his head. When Snickers reached his side she kept her head down and waited.

'So stroke her,' Jacob instructed in his quiet,

calm voice. 'Nice and easy. Tell her she's a good girl.'

'Good girl,' Rex said, reaching up and gingerly stroking Snickers' neck.

Keira watched it happen from outside the arena fence – the moment when Rex finally connected with his beautiful paint pony.

'That's called join-up,' Jacob said with a smile. 'It's step one in getting your horse to know and trust you.'

CHAPTER FIVE

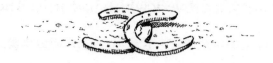

During the rest of Monday and the whole of Tuesday, Wednesday and Thursday, Rex kept to the deal with Keira and settled into working with Snickers in the round pen.

'Good, Rex!' Jacob told him when he sat quietly in the saddle and eased her forward with a squeeze of his legs. 'Keep your hands gentle on those reins, don't put any pressure on the bit.'

On Friday morning Keira, Brooke and Allyson

watched from the corral and saw how Rex was learning to relax and trust Snickers.

'It's been less than a week and we're seeing real progress,' Allyson smiled, going off to the barn to check the grain delivery which had arrived by truck.

Friday lunchtime, Keira saw that Rex had received an email from his dad. 'He's asking me how it's going with Snickers,' Rex told her.

'What did you tell him?' she asked.

'I told him good. And don't look so surprised.'

'I didn't . . . I'm not . . .'

'Yeah, you are,' he said with an embarrassed grin as he closed his laptop. 'To tell you the truth, I even shocked myself!'

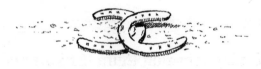

On Friday afternoon, Keira schooled Vegas in the round pen while Jacob worked with Rex and Snickers, demonstrating again what he meant by gentle hands. 'Even when you want Snickers to stop, don't do it all with a yank on the reins,' he explained. 'Do it by easing off with your legs and shifting your weight. See – that works better and it doesn't hurt her mouth.'

Rex nodded and worked on. At the end of the session he waited for Jacob to open the arena gate and rode confidently into the corral. 'Hey Keira,' he called over his shoulder as he left. 'How are you liking Vegas?'

'He's smart.' She followed Rex into the corral and dismounted. 'He learns real fast. Tomorrow I'm going to try him around a few barrels. Hey,' she added when she saw Rex stoop to unbuckle Snickers' cinch. 'What do you say we take these two out on the trail?'

'Now?' Rex straightened and glanced out along the meadow. The sun was low in the sky, casting long shadows across the valley.

'Yeah. We won't work them hard – just let them chill. It'll be fun.'

Rex started to frown and shake his head then suddenly changed his mind. 'Yeah, cool – let's do it.'

'Is that OK with you, Dad?' she checked as Jacob joined them.

'Sure,' her dad nodded. 'Why not take Rex up to Dolphin Rock, see if you can spot those elk?'

'That's a great idea. Only, don't tell Red Star I'm

taking Vegas on a trail ride,' she grinned as she hopped back in the saddle. 'He'll be totally jealous!'

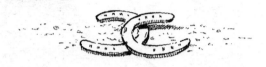

The creek gurgled across the meadow. They rode under a pure blue sky.

'I wish we had a meadow like this at Blowing Rock,' Rex told Keira. 'We have an indoor arena and everything, but this is way better.'

'Snickers likes it too.' Keira grinned as the cheeky paint filly lowered her head to snack on the juicy grass. She focused on keeping Vegas' attention on what he should be doing – trotting smoothly towards the Jeep road. 'Do you want to lope?' she asked Rex, who nodded. Soon they were riding fast and furious towards a big fallen tree at

the far end of the meadow, where Keira reined Vegas back with a soft 'Whoa!'

'How fun was that!' Rex sighed. His dark hair was blown back from his forehead and his skinny, usually sallow face was rosy for once.

'And how good were they!' Keira leaned forward to pat Vegas' neck. 'You see that smooth hump of rock a hundred metres off the trail? That's where we're headed. We should get there just as the sun goes down.'

'Do you really think we'll see elk?' Rex asked. 'It'd be cool – we don't have them in Sharman County.'

'Maybe.' Keira wasn't making any promises. After all, though dawn and dusk were the best times for seeing wildlife, the bull elk didn't like coming out into the open if someone was close by.

'If we see him, I'm gonna take a picture.'

'Cool.' Leading the way up the narrow trail until they reached Dolphin Rock, Keira put a finger to her lips. 'See the clearing and the aspen trees behind it? That's where I saw them last Saturday.'

She stopped talking and sat quietly, noticing that Vegas had flicked his ears towards the aspen trees and was listening hard. 'Sshh!' she warned Rex again.

Rex had unzipped his fleece jacket and reached for his camera from an inside pocket. *Zzzippp!* The noise unsettled Snickers, whose hooves clattered on the hard rock underfoot.

'Easy!' he muttered, almost dropping the camera as he tugged on the reins.

Ignoring him, Keira kept on searching the aspens. If the bull elk was in there, she would eventually spot his enormous antlers brushing aside the lower branches as he moved through the trees. *Yes!* She pointed to where the trees rustled and waited until the proud, beautiful elk walked warily into the clearing.

She heard Rex gasp and saw him drop Snickers' reins to raise the camera with both hands.

'Don't do that!' she warned, but it was too late.

The reins trailed on the ground, Rex pressed the button and his camera flashed in the dim light.

In a split second the startled elk reared, turned and bolted. Vegas spun away from the flash, lost his footing and began to slide down the stony hillside. Snickers reared on to her hind legs. 'Grab the reins!'

Keira called to Rex as she quickly brought Vegas under control.

But Snickers landed on one of her reins and trapped it under her hoof. Her head was yanked sideways. She reared again and as Rex grabbed the saddle horn he dug his spurs deep into her sides.

Snickers squealed – a shrill, panicky neighing sound. Spotting Vegas twenty metres down the steep slope, she whipped around and set off to join him, reins still trailing, Rex still hanging on grimly.

'Quit using your spurs!' Keira yelled. Snickers had laid her ears flat against her head, her nostrils gaped wide and foam began to appear at the corners of her mouth. And she was sliding out of control down the slope towards Keira and Vegas – there was no way of stopping her.

Crash! Snickers slid into Vegas with her full weight, trapping Keira's leg. She tried not to cry out in pain. Flung forwards, Rex clung to Snickers' neck, his face white with fear. 'What do I do now?' he begged.

'Wait. Let me try to grab her reins,' Keira mumbled. The pain was bad but she leaned sideways and reached down, counting on this, their only chance of getting both ponies back under control.

But again Rex panicked and did exactly the wrong thing – he used his spurs!

Snickers felt the sharp stab of pain, squealed and reared, whipping the loose rein out of reach. Then Snickers and Vegas began to slide down the gravel slope together, raising dust, crashing against each other, scrambling and sliding until they hit the fallen tree at the bottom of the trail.

Thud. Keira and Vegas hit the trunk with a sickening sound. The impact tossed Keira from the saddle on to the ground. She curled into a ball to protect her head, heard Rex cry out as Snickers crashed into Vegas.

Out of the tangle of bodies and legs, Snickers

managed to right herself.
By the time Keira had
uncurled, jumped up and
seized Vegas' reins, all
she could see was the
back view of Snickers
and Rex heading at full
gallop along the Jeep

road towards the Three Horseshoes.

When Keira bent down to pick her hat out of the dirt, she saw the bright red, gaping wound that had opened up on Vegas' back leg.

CHAPTER SIX

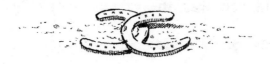

The stump of a broken branch sticking out from the main trunk had done the damage. Sharp as a spear, it had torn through Vegas' skin, deep through tendons right to the bone.

'I'm so sorry!' Keira whispered, taking off the pale blue shirt she wore over her T-shirt and folding it into a pad which she pressed against the wound. She used the sleeves to tie the pad in place.

Vegas twitched with pain but he stood patiently.

'Don't worry – I'll walk you home. Dad will know what to do.' Talking and working on the bandage, Keira managed to calm the injured colt. 'Let's hope Snickers didn't get hurt too,' she murmured. 'If she gets as far as the Walters' place, they'll turn her around and bring her home.'

Vegas lowered his head to nudge Keira's shoulder.

'I know – this sucks,' she breathed. At last she was ready to lead him slowly across the darkening meadow, limping as she went. She kept the barn firmly in her sights and whispered soothingly to Vegas that it wouldn't be long before they were home.

They were almost there, covering the last fifty metres when Brooke spotted them and came running. 'What happened?' she gasped. She held the meadow gate open as Keira led Vegas through. 'Where's Rex? Is Snickers OK?'

'Fetch Dad!' Keira told her.

But there was no need. Jacob had heard their worried voices and came out of the tack room into the corral. He took in the details – the blood seeping through the makeshift bandage on Vegas' back leg, Keira covered in dirt and limping badly. He ran to take the colt from her and told Brooke to get Keira into the house.

'No, I want to stay with Vegas,' she argued, trembling with a mixture of shock and relief.

Her dad nodded then ran for his veterinary bag. 'Ready – grit your teeth,' he warned as he unwound the bloodstained shirt.

Brooke winced at the sight of the jagged wound and Keira half closed her eyes. They watched as Jacob sprayed an anaesthetic on to the area then swabbed away the blood. 'Easy, boy,' he soothed. 'Let's see if you can bend the leg – good. And now take the weight on it – good again. No broken bones,' he told the girls. 'And the main tendons seem OK. The tear on the skin is ugly, but we'll stitch it once we get it good and clean.'

Keira and Brooke nodded. 'So what did happen?' Brooke asked Keira again.

Keira told her about Rex's camera and the way the flash had spooked not only the bull elk but Snickers and Vegas too.

'Brooke, hold Vegas steady while I give him a shot of antibiotics,' Jacob interrupted.

'Rex totally lost it,' Keira went on. 'He forgot every single thing he'd learned.'

'It happens,' her dad said, concentrating on giving the shot and stitching the wound before it grew too dark to see.

'But Dad, he wanted to take the picture so he just dropped his reins without thinking.'

'Not good,' Jacob admitted.

'And when Snickers spooked at the flash, what did he do? He only went and used his spurs on her!'

'Sshh!' Brooke warned. She could make out the figure of Rex walking across the corral on foot.

'Where's Snickers?' she demanded as he drew near.

'Yeah, Brooke – thanks for checking I'm OK!' he muttered harshly, brushing dust from his shirt. 'The stupid animal went crazy for no reason. I ended up in the dirt again thanks to her!'

'She threw you?' Brooke said.

'She ran right through the bit,' he claimed, making sure that Jacob was listening. 'I was doing everything to make her stop – using my weight, neck reining her in a tight circle – all that stuff.'

'B-but . . .!' *How could this be true?* The last time Keira had seen them, Snickers' reins had been trailing on the ground and Rex had been totally without brakes.

'But where is she now?' Brooke insisted, her voice rising.

'I tell you, she freaked out, went loco like all the other times.' Rex's scowl deepened and he refused to look Keira or Brooke in the eye. 'I'm going to email my dad and tell him this is it – Snickers had her last chance out there today.'

'But that's not what I saw . . .' Keira began to protest.

Rex's voice rose and he shouted over her as he stomped on towards the house. 'That's it – no more!'

'Leave it, honey,' Jacob sighed. He straightened up and shook his head as he looked at the pale moon rising. 'The first thing I have to deal with is calling Mike Martin to update him on the progress of his high-value ponies.'

'What will you tell him?' Brooke asked anxiously.

'That Vegas is injured and Snickers is missing,' he said in a flat voice. 'That we're in big trouble here and that's the truth.'

'Try not to worry.' Allyson sat on the edge of Keira's bed, looking out with her at the clear starlit sky. 'One night out on the mountain won't hurt Snickers. And tomorrow we'll ride out and find her, I promise.'

'She'll be all alone and scared,' Keira sighed. 'It gets really cold at night – it could snow!'

Her mom shook her head. 'Listen, honey, I'm more worried about you. How's your ankle?'

'A bit swollen, but OK.'

'You didn't eat any supper.'

'I know. I wasn't hungry.'

Allyson leaned forward to give Keira a hug. 'Try to sleep,' she murmured as she got up to leave.

'Mom . . .' Keira began then broke off.

Allyson hovered by the door. 'What is it?'

'I made a big mistake,' she said in a shaky voice.

Her mom came back into the room and sat down again. 'Tell me.'

'It's about Rex and the time last Sunday when we rode out with Reed.'

Allyson waited patiently for Keira to get to the point.

'Rex fell in the creek, remember? He said Snickers had bolted and thrown him off.'

'Yes, I remember.'

'She didn't,' Keira confessed. 'That's not what really happened. I actually saw him in the willows. He was beating Snickers up real bad – spurs and everything.'

'I hear you,' Allyson said quietly.

'What could Snickers do? She was in pain so she reared up and lost her balance. They both fell in the creek together.'

There was a long pause before Allyson spoke

again. 'And why didn't you say something when you came back home?'

'That's the mistake,' Keira sighed. Her bottom lip trembled as she thought of what had happened since. 'I made a deal with Rex. I decided to give him a second chance.'

'Oh, Keira, you shouldn't blame yourself for that,' her mom said softly.

'But I do,' she cried. 'If I'd told the truth in the first place, Snickers wouldn't be lost on the mountain. None of this would ever have happened!'

CHAPTER SEVEN

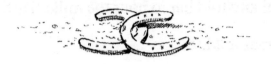

All night long Keira tossed and turned. Every time she closed her eyes, a picture of Snickers alone in the frosty pine forest flashed through her head – the poor paint pony alone and shivering in the dark, her head hanging, her whole body quivering from cold and fear.

In the morning, as soon as it grew light, she got out of bed and went downstairs to find her dad already up and dressed.

'Did you call Mr Martin?' she asked as she sat at the kitchen table. She ignored Popcorn, their ginger cat, who jumped into her lap and purred.

'I sure did,' Jacob replied. He gave Keira a bowl of cereal and told her to pour the milk. 'By the way, how's your ankle?'

'It's good, thanks. And what did Mr Martin say?'

'Rex called him first,' her dad frowned. 'Gave him all the usual stuff about Snickers spooking and going crazy. What was Mike going to do? Rex is his son, so he believed every word.'

'And?' Keira asked even more quietly than before. Popcorn gave up searching for attention, jumped from Keira's lap and padded towards the stairs to get a stroke and a fuss from Brooke.

'Mike said no way should we have taken Vegas

and Snickers out on the trail, knowing how mean Snickers can be.'

Keira shook her head. 'That's so not fair.'

'I know it. But that's how it looks to Mike Martin. He even said he wouldn't lose sleep if Snickers never showed up again, that she was more trouble than she was worth and so on. But then he calmed down and asked for details about Vegas – how bad was he hurt? Would he ever barrel race at national level? I told him it was too soon to tell.'

'Have you taken a look at him this morning?' Keira asked, pushing her bowl aside.

'No. You want to come with me?' Jacob took his hat from the peg.

She jumped up, winced as she put her weight on her sore ankle but still rushed to the door, opening it on to a dull grey dawn light.

'Jacket,' her dad reminded her.

Keira grabbed it and rushed out into the yard, limping ahead of him into the barn.

'Mike is sending his partner, Jeff Baker, to visit later today,' Jacob said with a worried frown. He followed Keira to Vegas' stall, turned on the light and opened the door. 'Apparently, Jeff wants to check out what happened to their two-hundred-thousand-dollar horses.'

Keira swallowed hard. She watched her dad kneel in the straw to examine the raw wound on Vegas'

leg. 'So I guess we'd better ride out and bring Snickers back before Mr Baker gets here.'

'The sooner the better,' Jacob agreed.

It was 8.00 a.m. when Reed and Wildflower joined Keira and Brooke at the entrance to Three Horseshoes Ranch. The girls had only waited for an update on Vegas before they'd saddled Red Star and Annie and ridden out along the Jeep road.

'The stitches held but the joint swelled up,' Jacob had reported to Allyson, Brooke and Rex, who was up but still in his pyjamas. 'And the whole leg is stiff. But that's pretty normal with a wound this deep.'

When Brooke had volunteered to join the search

for Snickers, Rex had backed off. 'I'll wait here for Jeff,' he'd decided.

He hadn't given eye contact as he'd slid out of the kitchen and back upstairs.

'He's feeling guilty!' Brooke declared, as Reed joined them by the gate. The morning was frosty and a stiff breeze blew down from the Black Pearl peaks so the riders wore thick scarves and gloves, ready for a hard search. 'Rex knows this is all his fault!'

And mine, Keira thought without saying anything. *If only I'd told Mom and Dad what I saw in the willows!*

'So let's find Snickers,' Reed urged. He was ready for action, not talk. 'Dad and I checked our meadows – there's no sign of a horse getting in with the cows. Do we know exactly where Rex made his involuntary dismount?'

Brooke smiled at the picture Reed conjured up. 'I asked him and he said there were no landmarks so he had no clue,' she told him. 'Keira, you saw Rex and Snickers heading in this direction?'

Keira nodded. 'Maybe they peeled off the track and back up the mountain. Or across the creek. Which way shall we try?'

'OK, let's think. Put yourself in Snickers' shoes,' Reed suggested. 'What does she do after she dumps her rider? She does what all horses do – she heads back to where she last felt safe, which is alongside another horse.'

'She goes looking for Vegas,' Keira agreed. 'But she gets back to the scene of the accident – the big fallen tree at the edge of our meadow – and Vegas is long gone. That's when she gets really scared.'

'And panics,' Brooke decided. 'She does the wrong thing. She heads back up the mountain.'

'To Dolphin Rock!' Keira cried. 'Which is where it all started to go wrong.'

'Good thinking,' Reed decided. 'We'll bushwhack off the trail, making sure we look out for tracks in the frost – let's go!'

They rode in silence, eyes trained on the ground as Wildflower, Annie and Red Star picked their way over fallen branches and between frost-covered thorn bushes.

'Elk tracks,' Reed said, pointing to marks on a

rocky ledge. The hoofprints were large and cloven. 'How neat is that!'

'I just saw signs of mule deer,' Brooke reported. 'Smaller prints and lots of them.'

But there were still no sets of horse prints with the telltale round metal shoes. 'We're almost at Dolphin Rock,' Keira said, pointing ahead. She

rode on, only reining Red Star to a halt when she reached the familiar clearing. Then she leaned sideways for a closer look at the ground. 'Hey, Brooke, Reed – what do you reckon?' she called.

The others joined her and found her pointing at a scuffed patch of frozen ground. 'Something pawed through the frost to get at the grass,' Brooke decided.

'And here's a fresh trail,' Reed said, heading beyond the clearing towards a bunch of pine trees perched at the edge of a gulley. 'These are good, clear prints!'

So they rode higher, following the trail through the trees, forgetting to look ahead until it was almost too late.

'Whoa, Annie!' Brooke reined her sorrel mare to

a sudden halt at the sheer edge of the gulley.

Keira and Reed stopped their ponies just in time. Below them was a drop of fifteen metres. 'What happened to the tracks?' Reed asked.

For a few moments Keira's heart plummeted. *Oh no – what if Snickers panicked so bad that she ran out of control, right over the edge? She might be lying down there in the gulley with a broken leg – or worse!* Then Keira got a grip – *no, Snickers is too smart, she wouldn't do that.* She steadied herself and started looking for more tracks. 'This way!' she hissed when she picked up prints that led along the ridge to a thicker patch of young pine trees mingled with aspens. But when she glanced over her shoulder, she saw that Wildflower's lead rope had uncoiled and got caught up in some thorn bushes and Brooke had stopped to help so she and Red Star went on alone.

They entered the dark thicket and picked their way through the trees, quickly losing sight of the others. 'Are we sure this is right?' Keira asked Red Star nervously. She seemed to have lost the tracks – it was getting almost too dark to see.

He stopped, flicked his ears this way and that. Then he walked on into the densest, most silent part of the forest. Above them, the branches of the tall trees formed a canopy, while underfoot, pine needles cushioned their steps.

A breath of air stirred the branches way above, a twig snapped under Red Star's hoof. Ahead of them Keira made out a shadowy creature. 'Snickers?' she whispered and edged closer.

The animal was hidden by reddish-brown tree

trunks but she caught glimpses of white, heard the swish of a horse's tail.

'Don't be scared, Snickers – it's me,' Keira murmured. 'Ouch!' She stepped down from the saddle on to her sore ankle and looped Red Star's reins around his saddle horn. 'Wait here,' she told him softly.

Calmly Red Star watched her limp on between the trees.

Keira held her breath. She heard Snickers trample the ground, seemingly trapped and unable to run. 'Wait – I'll help,' she promised.

She reached her at last, got her first clear view and discovered that Snickers' loose rein had hooked itself over a low branch. She must have reared and twisted but only made the situation

worse by knotting the rein around the branch. Now she watched Keira approach with fear in her eyes.

'I won't hurt you,' Keira murmured. She saw how Snickers had tugged at the knotted rein until the metal bit had dug into the soft flesh at the corner of her mouth, so she quickly began to unbuckle the bridle. 'How long have you been trapped?' she asked. 'Easy, girl – I'll soon have you free.'

Her voice seemed to calm Snickers, who stopped rolling her eyes and pulling away. Instead, she waited until Keira was done.

'There,' Keira said as she disentangled the trembling filly, uncoiled her lead rope and began to lead her back towards Red Star. 'We'll soon have you off this cold mountain and bedded down in your cosy stall, no problem.'

CHAPTER EIGHT

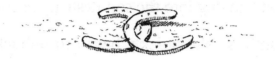

Keira kept her promise to lead the runaway safely back to Black Pearl Ranch.

'Good job!' Brooke told her when she saw Keira appear from the forest with both Red Star and Snickers.

'Yeah, her mouth's bleeding but otherwise she seems good.'

'Poor thing – she's shaking all over,' Brooke noticed.

'She's scared,' Reed said. 'No horse likes being alone all night and Snickers is still pretty young.'

So Brooke and Reed let Keira, Red Star and Snickers take the lead down the slope. 'Hey, and look at her belly!' Brooke groaned.

Keira stopped and bent down to examine Snickers. 'Ouch!' There were small cuts and trickles of dried blood in the skin where Rex had dug in his spurs.

'Yeah, he kicked her hard,' Reed sighed.

It was clear Rex hadn't learned anything about horsemanship after all. Sadly Keira shook her head and patted Snickers. 'Don't worry – this time I'm making sure Mom and Dad know what he did to you.'

Snickers sighed and let Keira lead her on across the meadow.

'Here's Mom, coming to meet us,' Brooke said, riding Annie ahead.

'Am I glad to see you!' Allyson greeted them warmly, watched them all get safely into the corral then took Snickers straight into the barn. She bedded her down next to Vegas, who poked his head over his stall door and gave Snickers a friendly snort as she passed. 'He says hi!' Allyson grinned.

'How's Vegas?' Keira asked, following her mom into the barn.

'His leg's still stiff but the antibiotics should deal with any infection in the wound.' As soon as she had Snickers in her stall, Allyson checked her from head to toe. 'What happened here?' she muttered as she stooped to inspect the small cuts on her belly.

'That was Rex.' Keira came out with the simple

truth. She still felt bad – as if she was the school sneak – but this was animal cruelty and it was easily top of her list of things you shouldn't do. 'He laid into her with his spurs – again!'

'I guess you're right,' Allyson agreed.

'I am,' Keira insisted. 'Rex had his chance, Mom, and he blew it.'

'I hear you,' Allyson sighed. She ran her hand through Snickers' mane and gave her a quick pat. 'Don't worry, the cuts will soon heal.'

'But what are we going to do?' Keira wanted to know, going up to Snickers and putting an arm around her neck. 'How can we stop Rex being mean to her?'

Allyson bit her lip. 'I need time to think about that,' she murmured. 'But right now let's be positive

– thanks to you, Snickers is back and she's warm, safe and happy, aren't you, baby?'

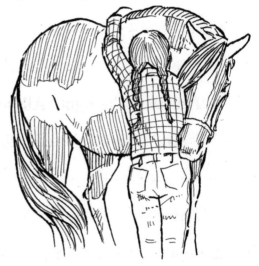

Snickers turned her head towards Keira and nudged her shoulder.

'Hey, it was nothing,' Keira laughed, hugging her some more. 'Red Star did all the work. It's him you should thank.'

Think positive – this was Allyson's take on life. Money was short, work was hard – look on the bright side. Who else could gaze out of their window at the white peaks of Black Pearl Mountains glimmering in the moonlight? Who amongst everyone they knew was lucky enough to train horses, compete in reining contests and live their dream? But as Jeff Baker's gleaming black limousine glided across the cattle grid and down the hill towards the ranch, Keira saw that even her mom looked worried.

'Tell Dad that Mr Baker's here,' Allyson told her. 'Say we'll take him straight into the barn to look at his horses.'

So Keira went to fetch her dad from his office tucked away behind the tack room. On the way there, she ran into Rex, who had already spotted the Lexus coming down the hill. His dark blue fleece jacket was zipped to the chin and the expression on his face was fixed, as if he'd closed down the shutters to keep everyone out.

'You know we found Snickers?' she checked.

'I heard,' Rex muttered. No thank you, no nothing.

'Mom saw the cuts you made with your spurs.' There was no point pussyfooting around – she wanted Rex to face up to what he'd done.

Rex shrugged and walked on. Lucky for him, Jacob stepped out of his office so Keira couldn't take it any further.

'Fasten your seatbelt,' Jacob warned Keira when he heard that Baker had arrived. 'We could be in for a rough ride.'

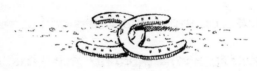

Jeff Baker was a small man with slicked back grey hair and a big ego. He stepped out of his car dressed in cream chinos and shiny brown loafers, with a soft brown suede jacket over a yellow sweater. 'Lucas?' he asked Jacob without offering to shake his hand. 'Mike tells me there's a problem with the horses. In fact, I hear that one escaped.'

'That was Snickers,' Jacob explained. 'She spent the night on the mountain, but my kids tracked her down and brought her back.'

'Show me,' Baker said, without so much as glancing at Keira.

So they all went into the barn and the owner took a quick look at Snickers before moving on to Vegas' stall. He inspected the bay colt's injury and an anxious look came on to his face. 'That's pretty serious,' he muttered then he fired questions at Jacob. 'A wound like this – how long does it take to heal? When do the stitches come out? Will Vegas still get on to the barrel-racing circuit?'

Keira's dad answered quietly and calmly, all the while keeping a hand on Vegas' neck to steady him. The message was – it was a waiting game. They would have to see how the wound healed before they made any decisions about Vegas' future.

'I suppose Mike told you what this guy is worth?' Baker quizzed. 'And the one next door. I put a lot of my own money into these horses. If Vegas' value drops, I'll be talking to my lawyers about lack of proper care at this establishment.'

Keira glanced at Rex. She didn't totally understand what Jeff Baker was saying, but the mention of lawyers didn't sound good. As usual, Rex blanked her.

'We're taking good care of Vegas and Snickers,' Allyson insisted. 'In fact, until yesterday our training programme was going without a hitch.'

'But today I'm looking at a colt with an injury to his leg and a filly who bucks, bites and bolts as soon as you look at her,' Baker argued. 'That can't be good.'

Rex nodded then spoke eagerly. 'That's right, sir. I told my dad – Snickers will never make it on the circuit. She's just too mean.'

Jeff Baker tutted and strode out of the barn with Jacob and the others trailing after him. 'So, Mister hot-shot trainer – give it to me straight. Mike says that Rex here is a great little rider and Rex is telling me that I wasted my money. Do you agree?'

Don't cave in, Dad. Tell him the truth, Keira pleaded silently. She glared at Rex as they came out into the corral. 'You have to speak up!' she hissed. 'Explain what really happened yesterday!'

Rex stared blankly back then shrugged. 'I don't know what you're talking about,' he muttered as he turned on his heel and stomped off towards the house.

So it's up to me, Keira thought and she stepped right in. 'Snickers isn't mean,' she told Mr Baker.

'Keira . . .!' Jacob's look warned her not to charge in and dump the blame on Rex.

She caught what he meant, frowned, then nodded.

'Sure, she's young,' Jacob went on. 'And riding a

filly isn't like riding a bicycle. They're not machines.'

'Sometimes they spook,' Keira added. And she began to hatch a new idea.

'You've ridden Snickers?' Jeff asked, noticing Keira for the first time.

'Yes, and Vegas. They're sweet – I like them both. Actually, I love them!'

'She didn't try to buck you off?' Jeff Baker asked doubtfully. He turned to watch Rex cross the porch and disappear into the house.

'I rode her in the round pen,' Keira answered brightly. 'We started at the beginning with her training programme – getting her to back up then moving on through forward walk and trot into a lope.'

'And?' The visitor was sounding more and more interested in what Keira had to say.

'She learns fast. She was great out on  the trail too, so long as she had a clear idea of what her rider wanted her to do ...'

Again Jacob shook his head in warning.

'OK, so we're ready to move on and try her round some barrels back in the round pen, aren't we, Dad?'

Jacob pursed his lips and looked thoughtfully over his shoulder at the open barn door. 'That's right,' he said slowly. 'That's the next step.'

'I could do it now!' Keira volunteered before Jeff

had time to think. 'Stick around while I take her

round the barrels, Mr Baker. Watch Snickers go!'

CHAPTER NINE

It was a huge risk, Keira knew. This wasn't the best time to face Snickers with her biggest challenge so far. After all, she'd only just come through the scary incident with Vegas and the fallen tree then she'd been freaked out by having to spend the whole night alone in the forest so she was sore and stiff. Besides, Keira had never tried her round barrels before.

'You're sure you can do this?' Jacob asked

quietly as he led Snickers into the corral and helped Keira saddle her up.

'Totally!' she told him. 'Snickers will be cool.'
Think positive – that's what Mom would say.

A few metres away, Jeff Baker stood talking with Allyson who had just come out of the house. Reed and Brooke were there too, busy rolling the barrels out from behind the tack room and setting them in a straight line across the middle of the round pen. There was no sign of Rex, Keira noticed.

'Remember – this is new to Snickers,' Jacob warned. 'Take it easy, don't push her too hard.'

'I know. I'll be careful.' Slipping a foot into the stirrup and swinging her leg over the saddle, Keira felt a tingle of excitement. It was the same feeling she had whenever she entered a competition ring with Red Star – the sharp fear that everything could go totally wrong mixed with the even stronger urge to ride and win. 'Thanks for letting us do this, Dad,' she murmured.

Jacob looked up at her and smiled. 'You have something to prove and I reckon you can do it,' he told her quietly.

'So let's go,' she said, reining Snickers towards the entrance to the round pen. 'Don't be scared,' she murmured. 'I'll take good care of you.'

'Good luck!' Allyson said as they went by.

Jeff Baker didn't speak but he wore an expression that plainly said, if this filly races around those barrels I'll eat my hat.

Snickers walked forward then hesitated when she

spotted the row of strange, brightly painted objects. Keira squeezed again.

'Our job is to weave in and out of these barrels,' she explained quietly, approaching them and letting Snickers take a good look. 'They're not going to suddenly fall over and crush you and nothing's going to jump out from behind them – OK?'

Satisfied, Snickers relaxed and Keira eased her into a trot. They completed a full circle of warm up then another before Keira pushed Snickers into a lope.

'Your pony has a beautiful gait,' Keira heard Allyson telling Jeff as she passed by. 'She's a class act.'

Perched on the fence, Brooke and Reed gave a thumbs up. 'You go, girl!' they called.

'Ready, Snickers?' Keira asked.

Snickers flicked an ear towards her rider, waiting for the next instruction.

So Keira reined her until she was pointing directly at the line of barrels and kept her going at a smooth lope, sitting deep in the saddle and looking straight ahead. Two steps away from the first barrel she neck reined to the right and squeezed with her left leg.

Would Snickers respond or would she crash straight into the barrel?

With split second, perfect timing the little paint made a flying lead change and swerved to the right of the barrel.

'Yeah!' Brooke and Reed cheered.

Now a shift to the left. Smoothly Keira reined the

filly and squeezed. Snickers understood. She made another lead change and a perfect swerve. The second barrel in the row of six flashed by. Now a weave to the right, and then the left, all the way down the line to the end, where Keira asked Snickers for a tight turn and got it. 'Now we go back the way we came,' she told her. 'And you get to do it all over again!'

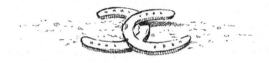

'She's a natural!' Reed ran to open the gate for Snickers and Keira after they'd completed the task. 'Dude, she flew round those barrels!'

'Good job!' Brooke exclaimed, holding the reins as Keira dismounted. 'Snickers, you're a star!'

'I knew you could do it!' Keira cried, flinging her arms round Snickers' neck.

Snickers was breathing hard after the flat-out run, but she took the praise with a satisfied whinny. And she swished her tail proudly as Jeff Baker joined them.

'I'm impressed. That was quite a display of horsemanship,' he told Keira.

'What about Snickers?' she asked nervously.

Baker gave a small nod. 'Rex was wrong – anyone can see that she has potential.'

'So we carry on training?' With one arm still around Snickers' neck, Keira held her breath.

'Definitely,' Jeff Baker confirmed. He shook hands with Jacob and smiled at Keira. 'I give you one more week to treat Vegas' injury and to turn Snickers into a true, top-flight barrel-racing champion.'

'Hey, Vegas, Snickers sure showed Mr Baker what she can really do!' It was later that evening and Keira was laying clean straw in the injured colt's stall. Next door, Snickers was chomping noisily on alfalfa. 'We set up a line of barrels and you should've seen her go!'

Vegas sighed and lifted his stiff leg.

'I know!' Keira murmured. 'You want to do it too. But you have to wait for that leg to heal.'

Just then she heard loud voices at the entrance to the barn and soon there were hurried footsteps and Rex's face appeared at the stall door. 'You made a fool of me, Keira Lucas!' he said angrily. 'I was watching from my bedroom window. In front of Mr Baker and everyone, you and Snickers made me look like an idiot!'

Keira gasped in surprise. 'I didn't mean . . .'

'Yeah, you did. You did it deliberately because you don't like me. You never liked me, right from the start!'

'Rex, calm down.' Reed had followed Rex into the barn and he warned him firmly.

'OK, you're right!' Keira ignored Reed and stepped out of Vegas' stall. Her heart thumped, she felt her face turn bright red with anger. 'I don't like you because you won't admit you're a lousy rider and you beat up your horse!'

'Keira!' Reed stepped in between her and Rex like a referee in a boxing match. 'You're not helping – OK!'

'He did,' Keira protested. 'I saw him. And Reed, come and look at these cuts on Snickers. Ask Rex how they got there – go ahead, ask him!'

'Both of you, back off. Take a deep breath, count to ten.' Putting his hands up to separate them, Reed did the counting. 'Rex, what else do you want to say?'

'Snickers is my pony. I ride her how I like,' he sulked.

'Even if you hack at her with your spurs and it means you can't do a thing with her?' Keira challenged.

Reed stared hard at both of them. 'Tell her how it really is,' he invited Rex more softly. Rex blushed and shoved his hands deep in his pockets. 'How it is back home – with you and your dad,' Reed insisted.

Rex scuffed his feet against the door of Snickers' stall. 'What do you mean?'

'Tell Keira how much you hate letting your dad down, how he has a certain look that says, "Boy, I expected more of you!" How you'd do anything to avoid that down-the-nose look. Go ahead – tell her.'

Rex hung his head. 'It's true,' he muttered with a catch in his voice.

'So actually, even if you have a problem riding Snickers, you can't admit it,' Reed guessed. 'You can't say, "Dad, I need help".'

Rex's head stayed down as he drew a deep sigh.

'So instead you blame Snickers,' Reed concluded. 'You're afraid to ride the horse so the only thing you can do is label her mean. It means your dad takes her to three different trainers and finally she ends up here at Black Pearl Ranch.'

There was a long silence then Rex sighed and said, 'How did you know?'

'It's a boy thing,' Reed said with a shrug. 'It's about a guy wanting to be flavour of the month with his dad, to be top dog and win all the prizes.'

CHAPTER TEN

'Reed was so-o-o cool,' Keira told Brooke. The sisters had got together in Brooke's room for one of their late-night chats and Keira was describing the incident in the barn. She sat on the end of Brooke's bed, her knees drawn up to her chin, with one hand massaging her sore ankle.

'Reed is always cool,' Brooke said with a self-conscious smile.

'But you should have been there,' Keira insisted.

'He guessed Rex was scared of his dad and the amazing thing was – he got him to admit it.'

'Yeah, I already figured that,' Brooke said, lying with her arms behind her head, staring up at the ceiling. 'We're lucky. It can't be easy having someone like Mr Martin as your dad.'

'What do you mean?' Rex's dad hadn't struck Keira as nasty or mean – just rich.

'Rex's dad doesn't do failure,' Brooke guessed. 'He figures Rex is just like him so he can fly to the moon if he wants to and he can definitely ride without needing lessons.'

'Jeez,' Keira sighed. 'I guess I never saw it that way.'

'That's because you care so much about Snickers you don't stop and think about the reasons people act the way they do. I'm not saying that's a bad thing,' Brooke added. 'But I'm glad Reed talked with Rex.'

'Me too.' Keira rested her chin on her knees. 'You know what he told him?' she murmured. 'Word for word, Reed said to Rex, "Stick with it, because Jacob Lucas is the best trainer around."'

'Yeah,' Brooke sighed happily.

Keira smiled. 'He said, "Listen and learn, Rex. Jacob will teach you everything you need to know."'

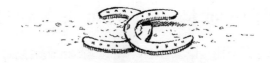

'Where is everyone?' Keira asked her mom when she rushed down for breakfast the next morning. The kitchen was empty except for Popcorn who lay curled on a chair by the window.

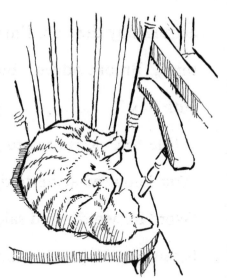

'Brooke's scooping poop in the corral and Rex is working with your dad in the round pen,' Allyson told her.

'Rex is working with Dad . . .?' Keira echoed. The sun had only just come up, there was still frost on the ground. She skipped breakfast and hobbled outside.

'Riding is not a battle between man and horse,' Jacob was telling Rex. 'As a matter of fact, if you want to turn it into a fight, consider this – your horse is a thousand pounds of muscle against your hundred and ten, so who's going to win?'

'The horse, sir.' Rex was standing with Snickers in the round pen, nervously holding the reins. Snickers looked edgy too. She was probably remembering the feel of Rex's spurs and his crazy, mixed-up instructions.

'Always the horse,' Jacob agreed. He waved at Keira and invited her to come into the pen. 'So riding isn't war – it's teamwork. And rule number one when you work with your horse as a team is to remember that a horse's instinct is to give way to pressure. You touch her with your right leg and she moves to the left – right, Keira?'

Keira nodded then held her breath as her dad got ready to help Rex into the saddle.

Be nice, Snickers! she pleaded silently. *Forget what happened last time Rex rode you.*

The little paint filly looked at Keira and whinnied gently. She looked so beautiful with her rich brown and pure white markings, so trusting and gentle.

'One more thing,' Jacob remembered as he glanced down at the sharp silver spurs strapped to Rex's boots.

'Sir?' Rex asked.

'Take off the spurs,' Jacob advised.

'Never think your horse is acting stupid.' It was Wednesday – four days before Mike Martin was due to pick up his son and his ponies – and Jacob was working with Rex and Snickers. Vegas had been taken out of his stall and into the meadow to graze quietly alongside Annie, together with Allyson's horse, Captain, and Jacob's grey mare, Misty. 'Every horse I know is super-smart,' Jacob told Rex. 'Smart enough to know that marshy ground won't take her weight even if a rider thinks it will, and that a big old bear could be hiding in the shadows of that pine tree on the ridge.'

'So always listen to your horse?' Rex checked.

'You're a team,' Jacob reminded him. He'd decided it was time to let him try Snickers around a row of barrels so he'd asked Keira to saddle Red Star and remind Snickers how it was done.

'Nice and easy,' Keira told Red Star as she loped him towards the barrels. 'This isn't an actual race.'

Red Star wove in and out, skimming the barrels without touching them, turning tight at the end of the row and weaving back. 'Perfect!' Keira told him, leaning forward to pat his neck as he flashed by the last barrel.

'OK, Rex – your turn!' Jacob called. 'Remember to neck rein and use your legs!'

'Go, Snickers!' Keira called as she waited with Red Star by the gate.

Rex sat firm in the saddle. He didn't hold the reins too tight, he didn't kick too hard. In fact he remembered all Jacob had taught him. And Snickers had already done this with Keira so she knew what Rex wanted her to do. She loped to the first barrel, felt the steady pressure from her rider's left leg and swerved to the right, then to the left and so on down the row.

'Your turn was a little loose!' Jacob yelled as Snickers went wide at the end.

Rex nodded then focused again – in and out of the barrels on the home run without a fault.

'Wow!' Keira rode up to him and gave him a high five. 'Get that turn right and before we know it you'll be giving Red Star and me a run for our money!'

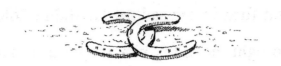

Thursday and Friday came and went. Rex spent every minute in the saddle, working with Snickers. Jacob took the stitches out of Vegas' leg and let Keira lead him down the Jeep road. 'He's healing well,' was the verdict when she brought him back to the corral.

Rex had just taken off Snickers' saddle after their last session in the round pen before his dad arrived.

'How did she do?' Keira asked as she helped with Snickers' bridle.

'She got the turn just right,' Rex said proudly. 'We cut three seconds off our best time.'

Snickers stamped and tossed her head then she nudged Rex's shoulder.

'You want an apple?' he grinned, taking one from his pocket.

Snickers bit into the apple with a loud crunch then Rex offered the other half to Vegas.

'Re-ex . . .' Keira began thoughtfully.

'Hmm?' Standing in the evening sun, with his Stetson tilted back from his forehead, Rex looked more relaxed than Keira had ever seen him.

'You know your dad gets here tomorrow?'

'Yeah, so?'

'So how about we have a barrel race – me on Red Star, you on Snickers?'

'With Dad watching?' Rex asked.

Keira nodded. The more she thought it through, the more she liked the idea. 'Picture it,' she urged. 'You ride her around those barrels and you show your dad that he bought the right filly after all. He'll have to admit – Snickers has turned into a total star!'

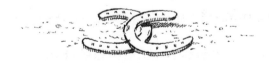

Rex took up Keira's challenge, but that night at supper he seemed quiet and unhappy. And he only picked at his peach and apple cobbler.

'That's *so* not like Rex,' Keira said to Brooke as they went to bed.

'I guess he's nervous about tomorrow,' Brooke said.

'No need,' Keira said confidently. 'Rex has worked so-o-o hard. Dad's taught him all the skills he needs. What's to be nervous about?'

'Everything,' Brooke argued. 'All Rex ever wants to do is impress his dad, remember, and tomorrow is the big – like, the *biggest* – test.'

'Yeah, I guess you're right,' Keira agreed as she stopped to knock on Rex's door to wish him luck.

He was sitting cross-legged on his bed, his laptop open. 'I just talked to Mom – they're in Chicago, on their way home.'

'So, why do you look so worried?' She thought

he looked kind of small and lonely there on his bed.

'Because!' he muttered, closing the laptop.

'Quit it,' she insisted with what she hoped was an encouraging smile. 'You and Snickers – you're the dream team!'

CHAPTER ELEVEN

Keira went to bed and slept soundly. She dreamt she and Red Star were barrel racing in a giant arena under a bright spotlight. Red Star adored being the centre of attention – he raced round those barrels and never put a foot wrong. Keira was stepping on to the platform to take first prize when a knock at her bedroom door woke her.

Her mom came into the room. 'Honey, did Rex

say anything to you about his plan for this morning?'

Keira fumbled for her bedside clock and saw that it was only 6.30 a.m. and barely daylight. 'Yeah, he decided to put in an extra training session before his dad gets here,' she mumbled, swinging her legs over the side of the bed. 'Why?'

'He must have got up super early,' Allyson said with a frown. 'He's not in his room. I just asked your dad to check the barn.'

Keira clicked into action. By the time she was dressed and downstairs, her dad was coming in from the barn. 'Bad news,' he reported. 'I didn't find Rex.'

'And?' Allyson prompted.

Jacob bit his bottom lip and frowned. 'I didn't find Snickers either.'

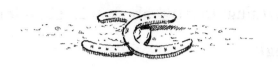

Everyone tried not to panic but they all knew this was a crisis. Mike Martin was due at midday so they had five short hours to find Rex and Snickers.

'He's scared out of his mind that he'll make an idiot of himself in front of his dad,' Brooke explained when she found out they were missing. 'His brain has turned to mush.'

'Poor kid. I had no idea,' Jacob said as he and Brooke set off in the truck along the Jeep road.

Allyson stayed in the house to call their neighbours and raise the alarm. 'If you see a kid on a paint filly, let me know,' she told them.

Meanwhile, Keira ran to saddle Red Star. By seven-fifteen they were out on Low Ridge trail, trying to figure out which way Rex and Snickers had headed. 'They know the meadow and the trail up to Dolphin Rock,' she said out loud. 'But I reckon they'll go further than that. Rex is fixated on getting away – he won't care where to or how far.'

Red Star had picked up the fact that something was wrong. He trotted strongly along the trail, listening intently, only slowing down when he spotted Tom and Reed Walters approaching in their empty cattle truck, on their way to pick up feed from Elk Springs. Reed leaned out of the window to talk to Keira.

'Are you looking for Rex and Snickers?' he asked without the usual greetings.

She nodded. 'Have you seen them?'

'Up on Navajo Rock,' Reed told her. 'Looked like they were heading out to Sharman Lake.'

'Thanks,' she muttered, reining Red Star off the trail and waiting for the Walters' truck to squeeze by. 'I'll explain later,' she yelled after them. Then she bushwhacked across country towards the landmark rock. Sure enough, she soon picked up signs of recent horse poop and hoofprints on the frosty ground. Red Star ate up the territory, surging through the bushes, ears pricked. A few hundred metres from the jagged pinnacle of Navajo Rock, he raised his head and gave a shrill whinny.

There was a faint reply.

'Snickers!' Keira breathed. Red Star whinnied again and changed course, heading over the ridge and giving Keira a view of Sharman Lake in the distance. Close by, between two tall, dark boulders she spied Snickers and Rex.

At the same time, Rex saw Keira. He turned away and urged Snickers on down the hill but Red Star was used to bushwhacking and he soon made up the ground.

'Rex, wait!' Keira begged.

The runaway shook his head and kept on going until she and Red Star drew level. 'Leave me alone,' he muttered, head down and refusing to look at Keira.

'Where are you going? How is this going to help?' she asked.

'I don't know. Just let me ride.'

But Keira and Red Star cut across his path. 'Come back to the ranch with me,' she said.

'I can't. What if this doesn't work out? What if I mess up?'

'You won't,' she promised. 'Anyhow, what's this if it's not messing up?'

Rex chewed his lip then finally looked up at Keira. 'You mean, running away? This is the worst thing I could do?'

She nodded. 'I'm right, aren't I? Honestly, Rex – you and Snickers can do this. Trust yourself. Trust Snickers. Come home with us, please.'

So this was it. Mike Martin's truck and trailer were parked in the yard and he stood by the gate with Allyson, Jacob and Brooke, watching Keira ride Red Star into the round pen.

Red Star trotted past the spectators, neck arched and ears pricked. When he saw the line of barrels, he put in an excited skip and dance.

'Easy, boy!' Keira steadied him and set him towards the barrels. *Go!* She squeezed and he set off like a bullet, swerved, swerved again, on and on.

'Go, Keira!' Brooke called. She held the stop watch to time her round the course.

Keira reined Red Star round the turn. He missed a beat, almost stumbled but quickly recovered for the race back.

'One minute twenty-six seconds!' Brooke announced as she pressed the button.

Now it was Rex's turn on Snickers. As Keira rode Red Star out through the gate, they rode in.

Snickers was high-stepping and dancing just like Red Star had been. Rex wore his dark hat low, shading his eyes. He didn't glance to the left or right, just focused on the barrels. He got his filly into position.

'Go!' Brooke yelled and pressed the start button.

Rex loped Snickers towards the first barrel. She tore up the gritty ground, kicking up dirt, swerving with split second timing – right then left, right again.

Mike Martin looked tense. He gripped the top rail of the fence and watched his son's every move.

'Good turn!' Jacob called. 'Keep her tight into the barrels – go, Rex!'

Rex reined Snickers this way and that. He wove her expertly between the barrels, cutting off a second here, a second there. He reached the finish line with a sliding stop.

'One minute twenty-three seconds!' Brooke yelled. 'Snickers wins!'

'So I didn't waste my money?' Martin asked Jacob as he watched Keira and Rex brush down their horses in the corral. His face gave no sign of any emotion.

'No, sir,' Jacob replied. 'With the right rider and a good training programme, Snickers is heading for the big time.'

'Hmm.' There was a pause – silence except for the sound of brushes working through manes and tails. 'The right rider?' Mike Martin echoed.

'In my opinion, that would be Rex,' Jacob said, looking his wealthy client in the eye.

Rex stopped brushing and took a deep breath. He hardly dared to look at his dad. Keira closed her eyes and waited.

'You're right,' Mike Martin agreed, and his face broke into a broad grin. He went and put one arm around Rex's shoulder, the other around Snickers' neck. He gave Rex the biggest squeeze. 'Son, I always knew in my heart that you and Snickers would make a great team,' he said.

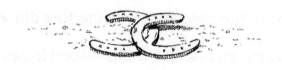

'So, Keira – give it to me straight.' Mike Martin had helped Rex load Vegas and Snickers into the trailer and they were almost ready for the drive home to Blowing Rock when Brooke took Keira to one side. 'Did you or did you not hold Red Star back on the bend so Snickers could win the race?'

Keira stared back, a picture of innocence.

'Tell me!' Brooke insisted. She'd seen Keira loosen the reins, watched Red Star hesitate then stumble.

Keira shrugged. 'Snickers did a great job,' was all she said.

And the sisters walked across the yard to say goodbye.

'Thanks for all your good work,' Martin told Jacob from the driver's seat while Rex did a final check on the bolts of the trailer door. He extended a hand and Jacob shook it warmly. 'I'll be telling all my buddies about your set-up,' he promised. 'You should get ready for increased business in the near future.'

'Sounds good,' Jacob grinned.

'Come on, son – jump in!' Mike called to Rex.

'The bolts are fine – go!' Brooke told Rex while Keira stood on the fender to peer in at Vegas and Snickers.

'We're sure going to miss you,' Keira told the horses.

Side by side in the snug, straw-lined trailer, Snickers and Vegas whinnied gently. Mike turned on the engine. Rex made his way along the side of the trailer. But he stopped and turned, came back to Keira and whispered the same question as Brooke.

'Am I right – you let us win?'

Keira shook her head and gave a wide-eyed, innocent look. 'No way! You and Snickers were the better team, end of story.'

Rex smiled. 'OK, I'm out of here,' he told her. And he smiled again and shook her hand just like his dad – firm and friendly. 'So long and thanks.'

The whole family watched Rex jump in beside his dad and waved as the trailer crawled out of the yard. They kept on waving all the way up the track to the cattle guard at the top of the hill. Then Keira sighed and walked slowly towards Red Star, still tethered in the corral.

'Don't say anything,' she warned, swallowing back the tears as she untied her pony. 'And I won't tell anyone if you won't – OK?'

What? he said with a gentle nudge and a low whinny.

She stroked his nose. 'I won't tell them that it was you who let Snickers win, not me. And I love you for it, Red Star, and I always will!'

Keira's home is **Black Pearl Ranch**, where she helps
train ponies – and lives the dream …

Black Pearl Ponies

GHOST HORSE

It's snowing in
springtime! Out
tobogganing with friends,
Keira spots a ghostly
horse and rider high on
the frozen mountain.

She's worried. Are the
mysterious pair on the run?
Are they even real? And if
they are, how long can they
survive in the icy wilderness?

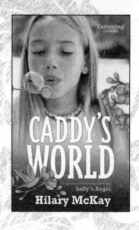